STORM RIDER

For my wonderful editor, Sarah

ORCHARD BOOKS
338 Euston Road, London NW1 3BH
Orchard Books Australia
Level 17/207 Kent Street, Sydney, NSW 2000

First published in 2010
First paperback publication in 2011

ISBN 978 1 40830 257 6 (hardback)
ISBN 978 1 40830 265 1 (paperback)

Text and illustrations © Shoo Rayner 2010

The right of Shoo Rayner to be identified as the author and
illustrator of this work has been asserted by him in accordance
with the Copyright, Designs and Patents Act, 1988.

A CIP catalogue record for this book is available
from the British Library.

1 3 5 7 9 10 8 6 4 2 (hardback)
1 3 5 7 9 10 8 6 4 2 (paperback)

Printed in Great Britain

Orchard Books is a division of Hachette Children's Books,
an Hachette UK company.

AXEL STORM

STORM RIDER

SHOO RAYNER

ORCHARD BOOKS

CHAPTER ONE

"It never stops raining here," Axel
Storm said gloomily. He was staring
out of giant windows at the dull, rainy
scenery that stretched into the distance.
"I mean, you practically need a wetsuit
and flippers just to go outside," he
sighed. "What if the rain ruins your
concert, Dad?"

"Ah, the fans won't mind a bit of rain," Axel's dad laughed. He was floating around the bubbly hot tub in their giant conservatory.

"This is the house I grew up in. There are always stormy skies here. That's how the band got its name, you know. I love stormy weather."

Axel's mum and dad were rock stars. Their band, Stormy Skies, had recorded twenty-two platinum-selling hits in eighty-three different countries around the world. They were rich – *really* rich.

In a few days' time Mum and Dad were putting on a huge concert at Prairie Plains, an enormous outdoor arena near the Soggee County swamplands.

The weather forecast for the big event was not good. Axel knew that if there was a real storm, the concert would have to be cancelled.

Mum looked up from her magazine. A sunlamp cast a warm glow over her beautiful face. "Axel's got a point, Storm. Think of all the money we'll lose if we have to call off the concert."

"Never mind the money!" Axel snapped. "What about all the disappointed fans?" Sometimes Axel wondered if his parents might be a bit *too* rich!

Just then, something caught Axel's attention. A silver balloon, about a metre wide, appeared at the bottom of the garden. It drifted towards them through the endless, miserable rain, and floated right up to the conservatory, where it hovered above the garden door.

"What the...?" Dad cried, leaping out
of the hot tub, dripping water everywhere.
Axel stepped outside to get a better
look. "Hey!" he said. "It's stopped raining!"

A fine web of sparks crackled around the balloon. It seemed to push all the rain away, leaving a dry area below it. A hatch opened in a little box underneath the balloon, and an envelope popped out with Axel's name on it.

The balloon turned away to leave. "Wait!" Dad yelled.

Axel and Dad ran after the silver orb, but it floated too high for either of them to reach.

"Here, jump up!" Dad said.

High on Dad's shoulders, Axel stretched out his arm.

He nearly had his fingers on the envelope…almost…just a millimetre more…and…*BANG!*

The balloon vaporised in mid air!

Dad yelped as an enormous electric shock hurled Axel to the ground. For a second, their hair stood up on end, then water cascaded from the sky, drenching them both to the skin.

Dad looked like a drowned rat!

Back inside the house, they opened the envelope.

The Old Gasworks
Hubble Bubble Highway
Airy Plains

Dear Axel,
I heard that Stormy Skies are
performing nearby, and that you
are worried about the concert
being rained off.

I have a top-secret plan that
you might be able to help me with.
Why not come and stay so I can
explain? It would be great to
see you.

Lots of love,
Uncle Taylor

"I might have known it was your Uncle Taylor," Dad grumbled. "He's been making hot-air balloons since he was nine years old."

"Cool!" Axel said as he fluffed his hair dry with an enormous towel. "Can I go and stay with him, then? I wonder what his top-secret plan is all about."

"I'm not letting you anywhere near Uncle Taylor, or his hot-air balloons," Dad growled. "You're bound to have one of your crazy adventures. No, you're booked in to stay at Celebrity Kids' Club."

"Oh, Dad!" Axel wailed. "Don't make me go there! You know I hate it!"

"Sorry, son," Dad said. "We can't look after you properly while we're performing. And you can't hang around backstage – it's too dangerous."

"Not as dangerous as Celebrity Kids' Club!" Axel complained. "Flamo the Fire-eater's son nearly burnt down my room last time I was there. And Brunhilda von Blitzen, the opera singer's daughter, insisted on singing at the top of her voice. I had to wear earplugs all week!"

"No more arguments," Mum said firmly. "We need to make sure that horrid photographer, Archie Flash, can't take pictures of you for *Celebrity Gossip Magazine* while we're busy. It's all arranged, and that is that!"

Newspapers, magazines and the TV all wanted pictures and stories about the Storm family. They had to work hard just to live a peaceful, private life.

"Fine! Have it your way," Axel said grumpily. "But we should still go to see Uncle Taylor. If his top-secret plan can save the concert from the storm, we should find out what it is."

Mum raised an eyebrow and looked at Dad. "Hmmm! Axel's got a point, again. What do you think, Storm?"

"OK, we'll go," Dad said. "But afterwards Axel's still going to Celebrity Kids' Club!"

CHAPTER TWO

"Your uncle was such a strange boy,"
Dad told Axel. They were in the Stormy
Skies luxury tour bus on their way to
Uncle Taylor's house.

"He used to make hot-air balloons
with granny's sewing machine. He
was always floating around in the
back garden."

"That'll be Uncle Taylor's place over there!" Axel pointed at a large silver balloon that floated over the damp, muddy countryside.

In the distance, dark stormy skies threatened. The weather forecast had got even worse.

The tour bus drove through a gate
and pulled up in the yard. A rusty
old sign announced that they were
at The Old Gasworks.

The bus hissed as hydraulic legs
sprang out of the sides, setting it in
parking mode.

The walls moved out sideways.
Inside, the bus tripled in size as it
became a spacious and comfortable
home away from home.

It was probably the most expensive
bus in the world. It even had a bath with
gold taps and a proper kitchen sink.

Uncle Taylor ran out to meet them. He had long hair and was dressed in old-fashioned clothes.

"Axel! My dear boy!" Uncle Taylor messed up Axel's carefully styled hair. "Haven't you grown!"

Axel sighed and smiled politely. "Hi, Uncle Taylor. Sorry we blew up the balloon you sent over. I was nearly frazzled when I touched it!"

"You weren't meant to touch it!" Uncle Taylor gasped. "It flies out of reach so you can't make a short circuit and damage it."

"It nearly damaged *us*!" Dad laughed.

Uncle Taylor looked up at the large silver balloon that floated over his house. The clouds seemed to melt around it.

"I've invented an amazing silver material," he explained. "It soaks up electricity from the clouds and creates an energy force all around it that pushes the rain clouds away. Thanks to that balloon up there, it never rains on my house!"

"That's why it didn't rain under the balloon you sent to us," Axel marvelled.

"Exactly!" Uncle Taylor was pleased. "I knew you'd understand, Axel. The larger the balloon, the wider the area that doesn't get rained on."

Axel's mum and dad looked at the darkening horizon. The huge storm was building. It looked like the concert was going to be a wash out.

"If we had something like that tomorrow, we wouldn't have to worry about the concert being rained off," said Axel's mum.

"That would be amazing!" said Dad. "And we could shine laser beams off the silver material."

"Could you do it, Taylor?" Mum looked really excited. "It would make it a concert to remember."

"It's possible," Uncle Taylor said.
"But it's a very big job. I'd need help.
There isn't much time."

Uncle Taylor winked at Axel.

Axel saw his chance. "I'm good with
my hands, and I've got nothing else to
do," he said innocently.

Uncle Taylor looked at his notebook and then at Axel. He sucked his teeth and said, "I could do it just in time...but only with Axel's help."

"It's not possible," Mum said. "Axel is going to Celebrity Kids' Club to keep him safe from photographers."

"I can look after him," said Uncle Taylor. "Who would bother to come all the way out here to take pictures?"

Axel smiled his sweetest smile. "Please, Mum? Think of the fans... You wouldn't want to disappoint them, would you?" Axel's parents were like putty in his hands!

"Oh...all right then," Mum sighed.

"Great!" Uncle Taylor smiled. "We'll have the balloon ready for the concert by tomorrow."

CHAPTER THREE

Uncle Taylor had an inflatable
workshop that seemed to grow out of
the ground like a giant blister.

Inside, it was light and airy. A long,
wide table stretched down the middle
of the floor. Cupboards and shelves
lined the sides.

"This used to be a helium factory," Uncle Taylor explained. "Helium gas is lighter than air, you know. Pockets of helium get trapped in underground chambers. It's made from radioactive uranium."

"Helium gas is radioactive?" Axel yelped.

"No!" Uncle Taylor laughed. "Helium is one of the safest elements there is."

"Phew!" Axel was relieved.

"There was a big deposit of helium under the ground here," Uncle Taylor continued. "There wasn't enough left for the factory, so they closed it down. But there's enough for me to fill my new balloons. Now," he said, looking at his young nephew. "We've got a lot of work to do."

Uncle Taylor sat Axel in front of a large sewing machine and gave him some material.

"This is an over-locking, under-locking, resin-filling seam stitcher," he announced. "As it sews the cloth together, it squirts a stream of resin into the seam, making it airtight. That stops the helium escaping."

He showed Axel how to press the pedal with his foot and make sure enough resin filled the seams while he pushed the material under the racing needles.

"No problem," Axel smiled. He lifted the needles up and removed his sample stitching. "It's easy – and a whole lot better than Celebrity Kids' Club!"

"You're a natural!" Uncle Taylor said, as he examined Axel's work. "There's only thirty more miles to sew – we'd better get going!"

Hour after hour, Axel fed the material through the sewing machine, checking the resin filler all the time. They couldn't afford to have any leaks in the balloon.

The workshop slowly filled up with the great pile of silver material for the skin of the balloon. Uncle Taylor tied a wicker basket to the material with hundreds of lengths of string. As they worked, Uncle Taylor explained the plan.

"Tomorrow, we'll fill the balloon with helium, tie it to my truck and float it over to Prairie Plains. If we go too fast, the balloon could escape or drag on the ground and burst. I only hope we can get there before the storm breaks."

Axel's fingers hurt, but he kept sewing. "Won't the storm blow the balloon away from the concert?" he asked.

"We'll use ropes and hooks to make sure it's secure," Uncle Taylor explained.

Soon after midnight, the job was done and the material was folded and piled into the basket.

"Thanks, Axel," Uncle Taylor yawned. "I couldn't have done it without you."

But Axel was already fast asleep, snuggled up under the balloon material in the basket.

CHAPTER FOUR

Axel woke up in a tangle of silver and string. His stomach rumbled. He was ready for breakfast.

"The storm is really building over Prairie Plains," Uncle Taylor explained as they ate their breakfast rolls. "We'd better get moving."

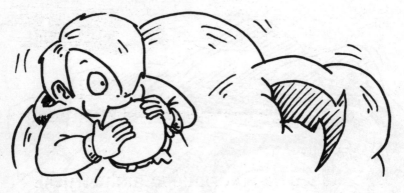

As the balloon slowly filled with helium, it began to form a shape that Axel recognised.

"It's a huge Stormy Skies sign!" Axel laughed as it lifted off the ground.

"I've put the ropes and hooks in the basket," said Uncle Taylor. "We're ready to go."

As they tied the balloon to the truck's towbar, a sudden voice behind them made them jump.

"Say cheese!"

Axel and Uncle Taylor let go of the rope to shield their eyes from the blaze of a camera flashgun.

Archie Flash, the photographer from *Celebrity Gossip Magazine*, had come looking for Axel!

"I knew something was up when Axel didn't arrive at Celebrity Kids' Club!" he grinned.

The rope whistled past Axel's face. It thrashed about like a snake as the balloon raced up into the air!

The rope had a mind of its own. It wrapped itself three times around Axel's leg and pulled tight. Axel felt himself jerked up into the air.

Now he was dangling from a balloon that was shooting up towards the sky!

"H-e-e-e-e-lp!"

"H-e-e-e-e-lp!" Axel screamed.

The world spiralled beneath him.
Uncle Taylor stared, open-mouthed in
horror. Archie's flashgun kept popping.
He had a great story now and he wasn't
going to miss getting the pictures!

"I'm doomed!" Axel squeezed his eyes
shut and imagined falling to his death.
"I should have gone to Celebrity Kids'
Club after all!"

Axel forced his eyes to open a crack. He was dangling ten metres below the basket. The sky swirled around, making him feel dizzy.

Suddenly, something inside him took charge. Axel felt brave and strong. If he was going to die a horrible death, he might as well die trying to save himself.

If I can just climb up to the basket, Axel thought, *that would be a start.*

Little by little, he hauled his way up the rope. His shoulders screamed with pain, but he had to hang on! He had to keep climbing!

All the time, the balloon was floating towards the towering black storm clouds at Prairie Plains. Axel clawed his way up to the wicker basket and tried to swing his leg over the edge.

He was getting weaker. He slipped. Axel imagined himself falling...

He swung his foot again and caught one of the ropes. Axel took a deep breath and pulled himself up a little bit more.

One big effort and...he fell into the basket. His arms felt like they had been pulled from their sockets, he was out of breath and panting, but...he was alive!

"Yee-ha!" he called out to the sky.

CHAPTER FIVE

Axel could see Uncle Taylor below him. His truck was following Archie Flash, who was hanging out of a car window, still popping away with his camera.

Axel was at the mercy of the wind. The sky was growing darker. The lights of the Prairie Plains concert twinkled ahead.

Thousands of people waited in front of the enormous stage where his parents were going to perform. The thunderclouds raced towards them. The sky had grown even darker.

"Ow!" Axel stubbed his toe on something hard and heavy. "The hooks!" Axel gasped. "I wonder…?"

A plan began to form in his mind. If the wind kept blowing him in the same direction, he would float right over the concert. Could he hook himself onto the scaffolding above the stage?

With one end of the rope tied tightly to the basket, Axel lowered a hook over the side like a fishing line.

The huge Stormy Skies balloon drifted over the audience. Someone recognised Axel and soon the whole crowd was staring skywards, watching the drama play out before them.

A huge arc of steel scaffolding
spanned the stage, supporting the lights
and loud speakers for the concert.

Axel was ready
with the hook...

...he was almost there...

...then...

...Axel felt the wind change direction.

"Oh no!" Axel wailed. "I'm floating away from the stage!"

Now he really *was* doomed.

Just then, a loud thropping sound made him look around. A helicopter hovered about twenty metres away. Cameras poked out of its doors.

Axel could see himself on the huge
video screens above the stage. He was
live on TV!

The blast of air from the helicopter
sent the balloon sailing back towards
the stage. Axel heard the hook clang as
it caught up in the girders.

"Hooray!" Axel cheered. "My plan worked! All I have to do is shimmy down the rope and..."

Cra-a-a-a-ck!

The first thunderbolt struck.

Cra-a-a-a-ck!

The storm had begun. Lightning danced over the surface of the balloon. Axel felt all the hairs on his body tingle and stand up on end.

Powerful fingers of blue electricity snapped and crackled outwards from the balloon, lashing the clouds, driving them away from the arena. Clear skies appeared above the cheering crowds.

Axel was stuck until the storm passed over. If the balloon touched the earth, it would short circuit and vaporise just like the smaller balloon had in their garden. Only this time, Axel would be vaporised too!

But Axel didn't mind waiting until it was safe for him to climb down. He had saved his parents' concert from disaster – and he had the best seat in the house to watch it!

As Mum and Dad began playing
Axel's favourite song, the crowd chanted
his name: "*Axel! Axel! Axel!*"

CHAPTER SIX

"It's nice to be home now that the rain has stopped!" said Axel.

Uncle Taylor had installed the Stormy Skies balloon over the conservatory. Dad was happy. He could still watch the rain and storms in the distance.

The concert had been a great success. Thunder and lightning raged all night, but not a drop of rain had fallen on Prairie Plains. The fans had thought Axel was in charge of the light show!

Axel's dad groaned. "We hardly got a mention in the papers for our performance. But there's a three-page story on Axel because he saved the concert from the storm!"

Mum sighed and hugged Axel. "I'm
glad you're safe and sound," she said.
"But when are you going to stop
having these wild adventures and be
a normal boy?"

Axel smiled. "I am perfectly normal,"
he said. "It's my family who isn't!"

CELEBRITY
GOSSIP
MAGAZINE

AXEL STORM lit up the sky last night, as his parents played a massive open-air concert in Prairie Plains.

Axel conducted the thunder and lightning to produce the brightest lighting display ever seen on Earth.

"GREAT SHOW, AXEL! WE COULD SEE IT FROM SPACE,"

said an orbiting astronaut.

Axel was not available for comment. His Uncle Taylor said, "That boy can really sew!"

By ace reporter, Archie Flash.

SHOO RAYNER

COLA POWER	978 1 40830 264 4
STORM RIDER	978 1 40830 265 1
JUNGLE FORTRESS	978 1 40830 266 8
DIAMOND MOON	978 1 40830 267 5
DEATH VALLEY	978 1 40830 268 2
SEA WOLF	978 1 40830 269 9
POLAR PERIL	978 1 40830 270 5
PIRATE CURSE	978 1 40830 271 2

ALL PRICED AT £3.99

Orchard Books are available from all good bookshops,
or can be ordered from our website: www.orchardbooks.co.uk,
or telephone 01235 827702, or fax 01235 827703.